# LITTLE BIG MOUSE

Written and illustrated by Nurit Karlin

HarperCollins*Publishers*

Little Big Mouse
Copyright © 1991 by Nurit Karlin
Printed in the U.S.A. All rights reserved.
1  2  3  4  5  6  7  8  9  10
First Edition

Library of Congress Cataloging-in-Publication Data
Karlin, Nurit.
  Little big mouse / written and illustrated by Nurit Karlin.
      p.   cm.
  Summary: A little mouse who wants to become big decides to find
out how to make that happen.
    ISBN 0-06-021607-7. — ISBN 0-06-021608-5 (lib. bdg.)
    [1. Mice—Fiction.   2. Size—Fiction]   I. Title.
PZ7.K1424Li   1991                                              90-36192
[E]—dc20                                                            CIP
                                                                    AC

*to*

**Robert Warren**

# A little mouse
wanted to be
big.

His brother was bigger than he...

but not by much.

His parents were bigger than his brother
and the little mouse wanted to be as big as they were—
or maybe even bigger.
He wanted to be really BIG.

He decided to find out
how he could make this happen.

The cat was napping.

But the little mouse didn't want
to ask *her* anything anyway.

He was going out to get his answer.

He couldn't even reach the elevator button,

but finally he managed to get in.

Waiting to cross the street,
the little mouse heard a heavy thump.

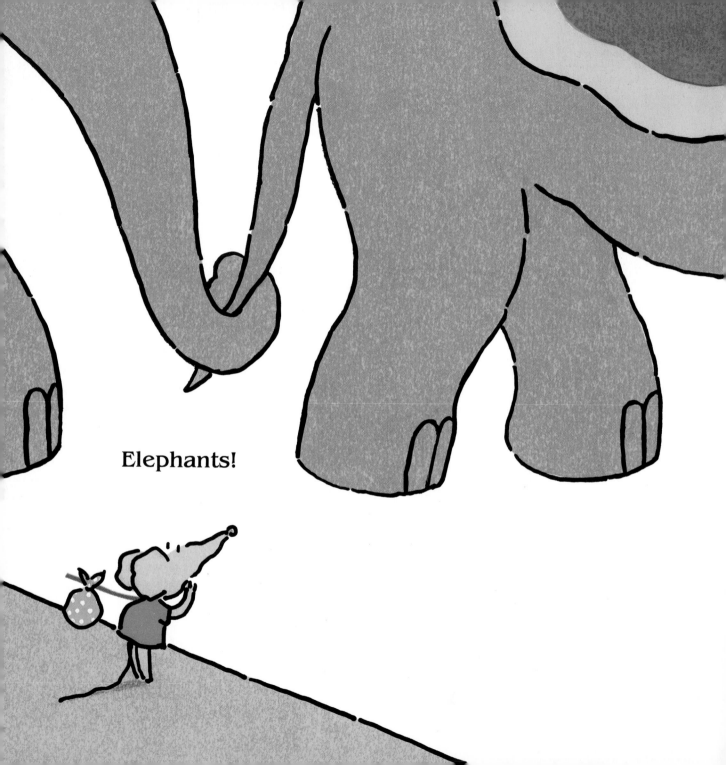

Elephants!

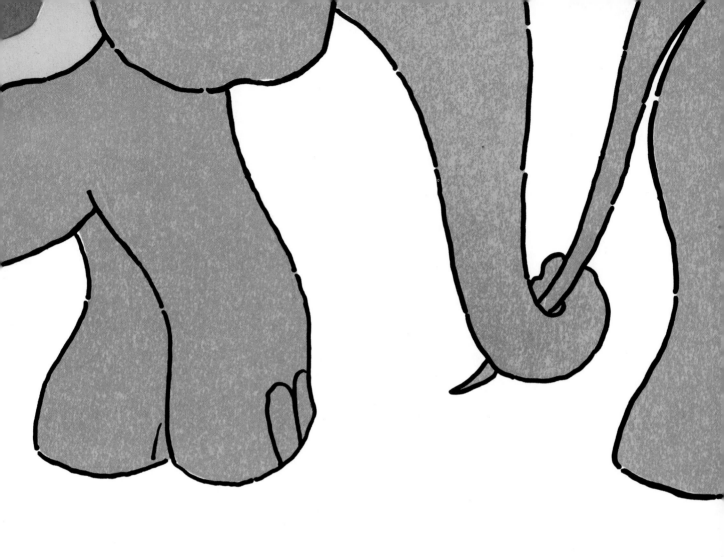

The circus was coming to town.

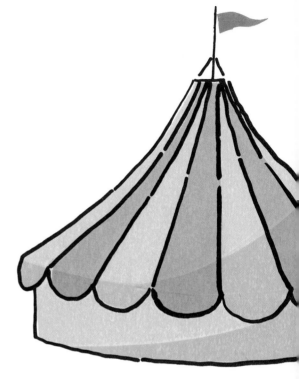

"Surely an elephant
will know everything
about being big,"
thought the little mouse.

He followed the parade to the circus ground.

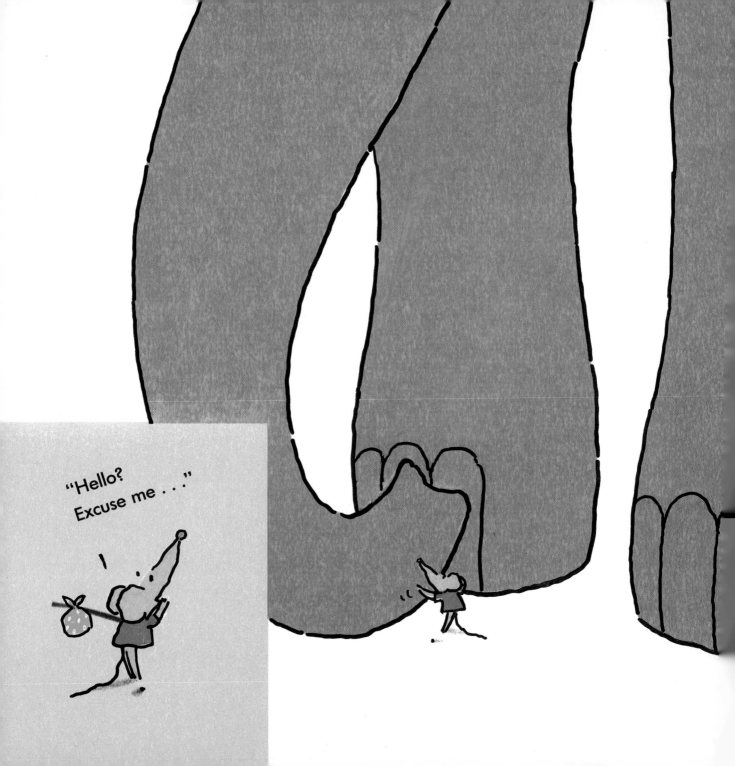

"I'm so little, the elephant
doesn't even notice me,"
he thought.
"There's one more thing I can try."

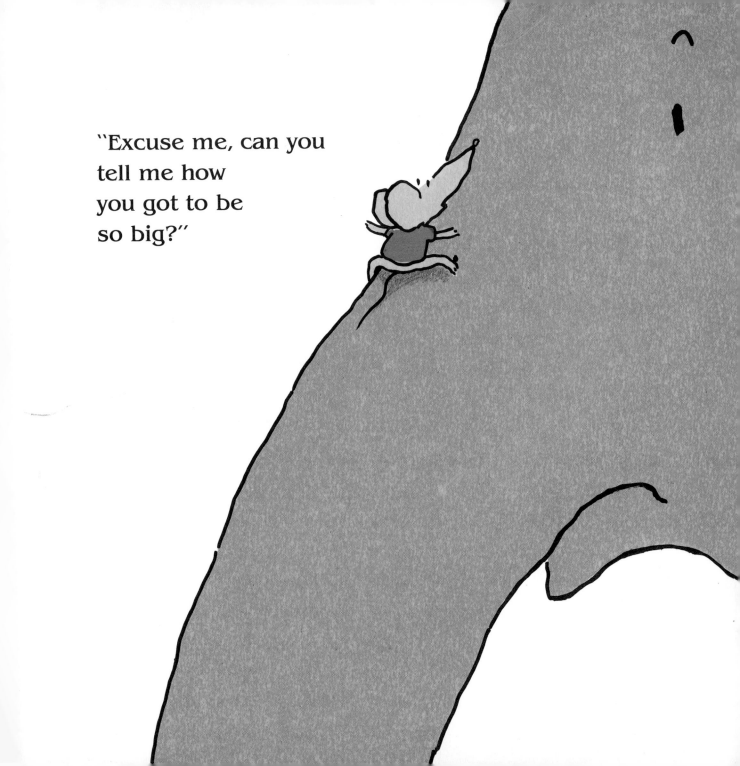

"Excuse me, can you
tell me how
you got to be
so big?"

"I'm not sure,"
said the elephant.
"I think I was
always big."

"I think I was big even when I was little."

The little mouse tried to imagine
what it felt like to be
really big.

His nose tickled.

"I think he was always big,"
said the elephant.

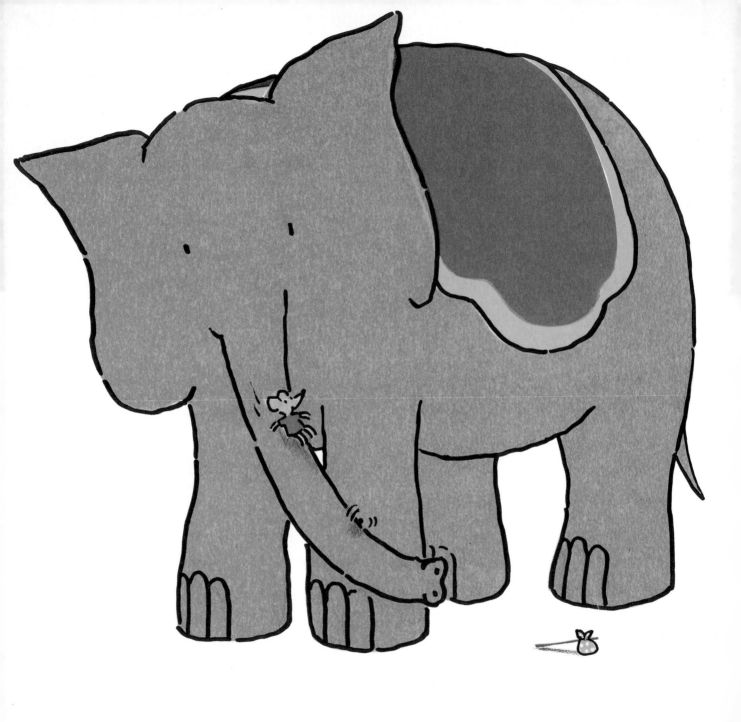

It was late
and time for supper.
Little Big Mouse said good-bye
to his friends
and hurried home.

Everybody was already at the table.
"You're late," his father said.
His brother snickered.
"Eat your soup," said his mother,
"and you'll grow to be big."

But
the little mouse
ate it
because he was
hungry.